JEAN DE BRUNHOFF

THE STORY
OF
BABAR

the little elephant

Translated from the French by Merle Haas
Harrison Smith and Robert Haas
New York ··············1933
Dragonfly Books • Alfred A. Knopf

In the same series:

The Travels of Babar
Babar the King

Dr. M. Jerry Weiss, Distinguished Service Professor of Communications at Jersey City State College, is the educational consultant for Dragonfly Books. A past chair of the International Reading Association President's Advisory Committee on Intellectual Freedom, he travels frequently to give workshops on the use of trade books in schools.

Library of Congress Cataloging-in-Publication Data

Brunhoff, Jean de, 1899–1937.

The story of Babar, the little elephant.

Translation of: Histoire de Babar, le petit éléphant.

Summary: An orphaned baby elephant goes to live in the city with an old lady who gives him everything he wants, but eventually returns to the forest where he is crowned king of the elephants.   ISBN 0-394-82940-9 (pbk.) ISBN 0-394-80575-5 (trade) ISBN 0-394-86823-4 (fac.) ISBN 0-394-90575-X (lib. bdg.)

[1. Elephants—Fiction]   I. Title.

PZ7.B828428St   1984   [E]   84-3308

First Dragonfly edition: October 1989

Manufactured in the United States of America

1   2   3   4   5   6   7   8   9   10

In the great forest
a little elephant is born.
His name is Babar.
His mother loves him very much.
She rocks him to sleep
with her trunk
while singing softly to him.

Babar has grown bigger. He now pla
He is a very good little elephant.   See hi

th the other little elephants.
ging in the sand with his shell.—

Babar is riding happily
on his mother's back,
when a wicked hunter,
hidden behind some bushes,
shoots at them.

The hunter has killed Babar's mother!
The monkey hides, the birds fly away,
Babar cries.
The hunter runs up to catch
poor Babar.

Babar runs away
because he is afraid
of the hunter.
After several days,
very tired indeed,
he comes to a town...

He hardly knows what to make of it
    because
this is the first time
    that he has seen
    so many houses.

So many things are new to him!
The broad streets!
The automobiles and buses!
However, he is especially interested
in two gentlemen
he notices on the street.

He says to himself:
«Really they are very well dressed.
I would like to have
some fine clothes, too!
I wonder how I can get them ???»

Luckily,
a very rich old lady
who has always been fond
of little elephants
understands right away
that he is longing
for a fine suit.
As she likes to make people happy,
she gives him
her purse.

Babar says to her politely:
« Thank you, Madam. »

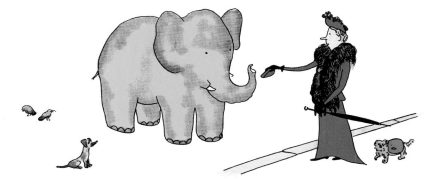

Without wasting any time,
Babar goes into a big store.
He enters the elevator.
It is such fun
to ride up and down
in this funny box,
that he rides all the way up ten times
and all the way down ten times.
He did not want to stop
but the elevator boy finally said to him :
" This is not a toy,
Mr. Elephant.
You must get out
and do your shopping.
Look,
here is the floorwalker. ”

a
shirt
with a collar
and
tie,

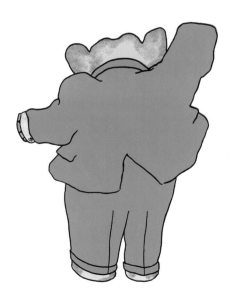

a suit
of a
becoming
shade of
green,

ruys himself :

then
a
handsome
derby
hat,

and
also
shoes
with
spats.

Well satisfied
with his purchases
and feeling
very elegant indeed,
Babar now goes
to the photographer
to have his picture taken.

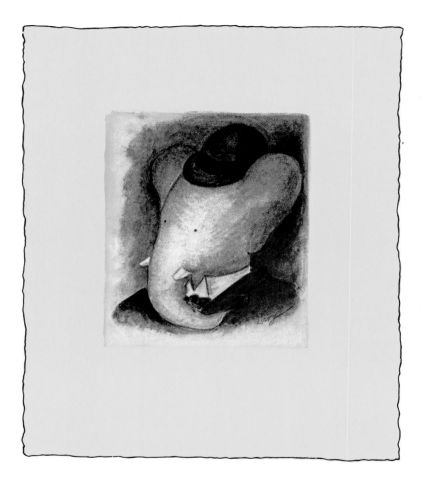

And here is his photograph.

Babar dines
with his friend the old lady.
She thinks he looks very smart
in his new clothes.
After dinner, because he is tired,
he goes to bed
and falls asleep very quickly.

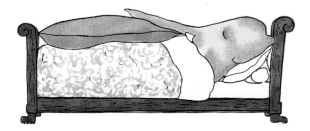

Babar now lives
at the old lady's house.
In the mornings,
he does setting-up exercises with her,
and then he takes
his bath.

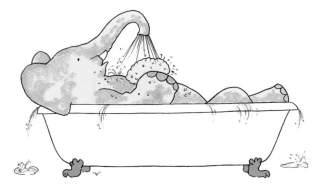

te goes out for an automobile ride every day.
  The old lady has given him the car.
  She gives him whatever he wants. —

A learned professor gives him lessons.
Babar pays attention
and does well in his work.
He is a good pupil and makes rapid progress.

In the evening, after dinner,
He tells the old lady's friends
All about his life in the great forest.—

However,
Babar is not quite happy,
for he misses playing
in the great forest
with his little cousins
and his friends the monkeys.

He often stands at the window,
thinking sadly of his childhood,
and cries
when he remembers
his Mother.

Two years have passed.
One day during his walk
he sees two little elephants
coming toward him.
They have no clothes on.
"Why," he says in astonishment to the old lady,
"It's Arthur and Céleste, my little cousins!"

Babar kisses them affectionately and hurries off with them to buy them some fine clothes.

He takes them to a pastry shop
to eat some good cakes.

Meanwhile the elephants are calling and hunt and their moth Fortunately, in flying over the tou and comes back qui

Arthur

Celeste

Celeste

Arthur

the forest,
and low for Arthur and Céleste,
very worried.
old marabou bird has seen them
tell the news.

The mothers of Arthur and Céleste
have come to the town to fetch them.
They are very happy to have them back,
but they scold them just the same
because they ran away.

Babar makes up his mind to go back
with Arthur and Céleste and their mothers
to see the great forest again.
The old lady helps him
to pack his trunk.

They are all ready to start.
Babar kisses the old lady good-bye.
He would be quite happy to go
if it were not for leaving her.
He promises to come back some day.
He will never forget her.

They have gone...
There is no room
    in the car
  for the mothers,
 so they run behind,
and lift up their trunks
to avoid breathing the dust.
  The old lady
  is left alone.
      Sadly
    she wonders:

« When shall I see my little Babar again ? »

Alas, that very day, the King of the elephants
had eaten a bad mushroom.

It poisoned him and he became ill,
so ill that he died.
This was a great calamity.

After the funeral
the three oldest elephants were holding a meeting
to choose a new King.

Just then they hear a noise, t...
Guess what they see! Babar arriving
and all the elephants running and shout...

"Here they are!
Here they are!
Hello Babar! Hello Arthur!
Hello Céleste!
What beautiful clothes!
What a beautiful car!"

urn around.
n his car,

Then Cornelius,
the oldest of all the elephants,
spoke in his quavering voice:
"My good friends, we are seeking a King,
why not choose Babar?
He has just returned from the big city,
he has learned so much living among men,
let us crown him King."
All the other elephants thought that
Cornelius had spoken wisely—
and eagerly they await
Babar's reply.

"I want to thank you one and all,"
said Babar,
"but before accepting your proposal,
I must explain to you
that, while we were travelling in the car,
Céleste and I
became engaged.
If I become your King, she will be your Queen."

Long live Queen Céleste!

Long live King Babar!!!
cry all the elephants without a moment's hesitation.
And thus it was that Babar became King—

"You have good ideas,"
said Babar to Cornelius,
"I will therefore make you a general,
and when I get my crown,
I will give you my hat.
In a week
I shall marry Céleste.
We will then have a splendid party
in honor of our marriage
and our coronation."
Then turning to the birds, Babar asks them
to go and invite all the animals to the festivities,

and he tells the dromedary to go to the town
and buy some beautiful wedding clothes.

The wedding guests begin to arrive.
The dromedary returns with the bridal costumes
just in the nick of time for the ceremony.

After the wedding and the coronatio

rybody dances merrily.

The festivities are over,
night has fallen,
the stars have risen in the sky.
King Babar and Queen Céleste
are indeed
very happy.

Now the world is asleep.
The guests have gone home—
  happy, though tired
  from too much dancing.
They will long remember
this great celebration.—

And now King Babar and Queen Céleste,
both eager for further adventures,
set out on their honeymoon
in a gorgeous yellow balloon. —